Ten in the Bed

for Felice
J.C.

First published in Great Britain in 2006 by Gullane Children's Books
This paperback edition published 2007 by

Gullane Children's Books
185 Fleet Street, London, EC4A 2HS
www.gullanebooks.com

3 5 7 9 10 8 6 4 2

Text and illustrations © Jane Cabrera 2006

The right of Jane Cabrera to be identified as the author and illustrator of this work has
been asserted by her in accordance with the copyright, Designs and Patents Act, 1988.
A CIP record for this title is available from the British Library.

ISBN: 978-1-86233-651-3

Printed and bound in China

Ten in the Bed

by Jane Cabrera

GULLANE CHILDREN'S BOOKS

Here is the **Little One**
A tired and sleepy head.
Stretching and yawning
He's ready for bed.

But...

10

There were **ten** in the bed
And the **Little One** said,
"**M**ove over, move over."

So they all rolled over
And the **Snorer**
fell out.

9 There were **nine** in the bed
And the **Little One** said,
"Move over, move over."

So they all rushed over
And the **Cook fell out.**

There were **eight** in the bed
And the **Little One** said,
"Move over, move over."

So they all bounced over
And the **Trumpeter fell out.**

7

There were **SEVEN** in the bed
And the **Little One** said,
"**Move** over, move over."

So they all groaned over
And the **Doctor**
fell out.

There were **six** in the bed
And the Little One said,
"Move over, move over."

So they all leaped over
And the **Ballerina fell out.**

5

There were **five** in the bed
And the **Little One** said,
"Move over, move over."

So they all swayed over
And the **Pirate fell out.**

4

There were **four** in the bed
And the **Little One** said,
"Move over, move over."

So they all bowed over
And the **Princess fell out.**

2

There were **TWO** in the bed
And the **Little One** said,
"Move over, move over."
So the Astronaut floated over
And **she fell out.**

There was **one** in the bed
And **everyone** said,
"Move over, move over."

So he moved over
And he...

...they all danced about!
Then the **Little One** screamed
And he gave a big shout...

So they all settled down and went to sleep.
There was not a sound, there was not a peep.
Until the Little One said . . .

"Goodnight!"